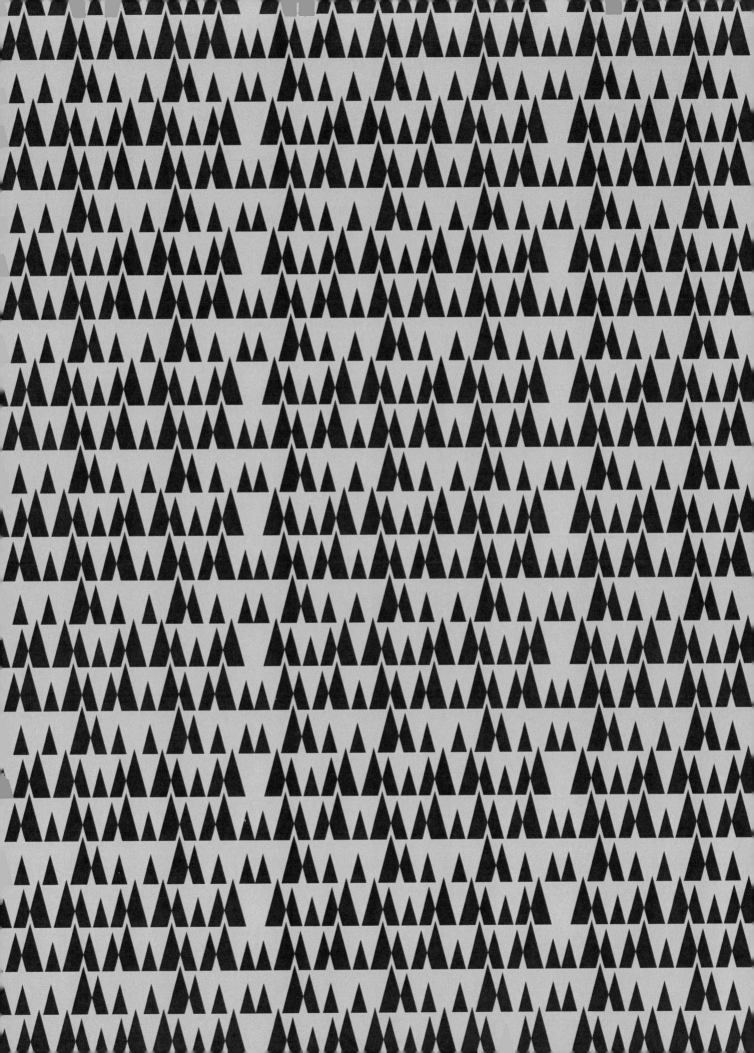

THE
MITTEN
THIEF

A Story by
Jill Kaufenberg

ISBN: 979-8-9850242-6-5
Library of Congress Control Number: Pending
Printed in the United States of America
First Printing: 2022

Published by Publish Her, LLC
2909 South Wayzata Boulevard
Minneapolis, MN 55405
www.publishherpress.com

PUBLISH **HER**™

To my inspiration and winter lovers:
Finley, Kye, Talia and Justin

And to the snow angels and snowball slingers,
the igloo builders, sledders and ski-run shredders,
the queens of the mountain and kings of the rink,
from crisp mornings at the bus stop to long nights around the bonfire,
in flurries and polar winds, squalls and snowmageddon,
we stand with winter kids, at home outside whatever the weather.

MORE SNOW?!

Molly and her sister Jules wake up late. Outside, all they see is snow. For days, they had sledded and sculpted, tossed and tunneled until their fingers and faces were numb. Now a fresh blanket covers the ground. Ten fluffy inches. Maybe more.

It's nearly 9 o'clock. Surely their friends are in snow boots already.

LAST ONE OUT IS A FROZEN EGG!

Molly bounds downstairs, her little sister hot on her heels.

They hear Dad holler:

IT'S A COLD ONE! BRING YOUR GOOD MITTENS!

That's when Molly remembers. Yesterday her mitten went missing.
She searched all afternoon and into the twilight. But no mitten.
With no one looking, Molly grabs Mom's favorite pair.

NO WAY I'M LOSING THESE!

The wind whooshes. The door slams. Outside at last!
Tugging on her hat, Molly hears laughter. It's their
friends—Max, Addie and Noah.

And then they notice something odd.

Their friends all have mismatched mittens. Noah lost one sledding. Addie's went missing in a snow fort. Max dropped one for just a second or two.

LOOK!

Jules says, wiggling her fingers.
She might be the youngest. But at
least her mittens match.

Up the sledding hill they go. The big kids move too fast for little Jules. Her face is cold. Her boots and hood are heavy with snow.

WHY CAN'T MOLLY WAIT **FOR ONCE?**

This morning's snow is wet and sticky,
perfect for making snowballs.

Noah lobs one Molly doesn't see coming. A direct hit!
She takes off a mitten to wipe snow from her eyes.

At that moment, something happens. So quick and so quiet that no one notices. One second it's there. The next it's gone!

HOOOOOOOLD IT! WHERE IS MY MITTEN?!

Jules snaps to attention. She sees something that surprises her. In the fresh snow, something almost too small to notice—unless you're small, too.

And then ...

Does Jules see ...

... what she thinks she sees?

It's Mom's mitten, plain as day. But it's zigging and zagging on two tiny legs!

In a flash, Jules is on her feet, racing over snow-covered humps.
She closes in with a flying leap.

GOTCHA!

Jules catches her breath. As she loosens her grip, the mitten jiggles and wiggles. Out slides an unbelievable sight. Before her stands a strange spiky creature, no bigger than her hand.

THAT'S NOT YOUR MITTEN!

The Mitten Thief begins to shiver. It looks so small and cold.
Jules can relate. Lowering Mom's mitten, she lets the creature
crawl back inside.

In front of them looms Snow Mountain, where the plow pushes ice and snow and whatever's in its path. Some years it doesn't melt until May. The Mitten Thief scrambles up the ice. Jules trails behind, careful not to slip. At the top, they wait.

WHAT IN THE WORLD?

A hole in the mountain opens, and with a wink the Mitten Thief disappears. Without thinking, Jules jumps in too.

Down Jules slides, landing with a soft thud. Her eyes
take a moment to adjust. What is she seeing?

Shimmering light. Polished ice. Colorful blankets tied up
with old scarves. Atop a snowdrift stands the Mitten Thief.
Jules sees they are not alone.

Back at the sledding hill, Molly looks up. Where on earth did Jules go? Losing Mom's mitten is bad. Losing her sister is much worse.

Inside Snow Mountain, a crowd gathers around Jules.
The Mitten Thieves nod and smile, cozy in their borrowed
mittens. Is that Noah's? And Max's and Molly's?

The sun begins to flood through the window. Jules sees the Mitten Thieves jump into action, turning cranks and pushing buttons.

As they do, the clouds move in, and the sky fills with fluffy flakes.
Jules hears Molly calling her name from outside.

The mystery of the missing mittens is a mystery no longer.

CAN THIS **BE REAL?** THEY'RE MAKING IT SNOW
SO WE **LOSE OUR MITTENS!**

The friends huddle. They need their stolen mittens, on this they agree. But how? The Mitten Thieves may freeze without them.

Jules has an idea—the lost and found at the school. They whisper.
They plan. They climb down Snow Mountain and move into action.

When Addie and Max return, their sled is piled high with one-off mittens. Lost and never claimed. All colors, sizes and styles. Word travels fast. Soon all the neighbor kids arrive.

The creatures climb down Snow Mountain one by one. As they do, an owner steps up to claim their mitten. Then a perfect replacement is given to each Mitten Thief from the box.

Last in line is Molly's Mitten Thief.
There are no replacements left.
It returns Molly's mitten with a hopeful look.

Jules notices the little
thief shiver. She slides
off her precious mitten.

FOR YOU.

The Mitten Thief smiles
broadly. It slips into the
mitten. A perfect fit.

The snowfall dwindles. Patches of blue sky appear. No need
for snowmaking, at least for a while. As Molly and Jules
burst in from the cold, Mom and Dad are waiting.

WHERE HAVE YOU BEEN?
JULES, WHERE IS YOUR MITTEN?

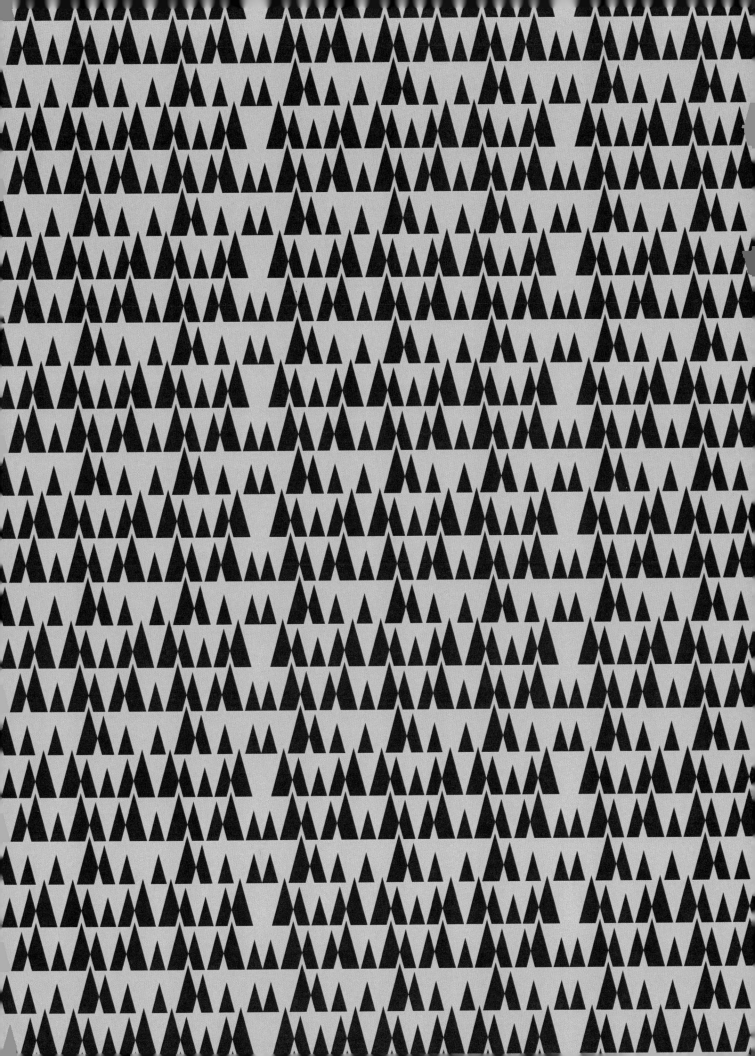

Made in the USA
Columbia, SC
27 October 2022